T0368421

The Box of Imagination

Elizabeth Marshall

Cecelia Smith

Illustrated by: Elizabeth Marshall & Elisa Lorraine Yeto

To order additional copies of this book, contact:
Xlibris
844-714-8691
www.Xlibris.com
Orders@Xlibris.com

ISBN: Softcover   979-8-3694-2035-5
        Hardcover   979-8-3694-2071-3
        EBook   979-8-3694-2036-2

Library of Congress Control Number: 2024908038

Print information available on the last page

Rev. date: 04/30/2024

Years ago, my sister Cele gave me ideas to create a book for children that would be worth publishing. At that time, I was taking a two year course in children's literature, and she knew I had passion for writing and illustrating. I worked on it from time to time but, it wasn't enough so I put it aside. The years passed and I finally decided it was time to turn her ideas into this story.

It was an interesting journey for me. The more I wrote the more my own ideas came to me. I also discovered that words are the tools that authors use to form images in the mind of the reader and the writer. And as I wrote, the images that entered into my mind became the illustrations in this book.

Imagination is wonderful!

Although Cele is no longer with us, I thank her for pulling me into this opportunity and planting the seed in my mind. I'd also like to thank Darlene and Lyle for their support and enthusiasm as it took me many hours. Lastly, I would like to thank the folks at Xlibris Publishing for believing in my writing, my illustrations, and making it all happen.

In memory of my sister Cele

It was a stormy November day. Elizabeth and Jason looked out their window at the pouring rain and swaying trees. Leaves swirled in the air. They'd planned to try out their new swing set and ride their bikes today, but the storm kept them inside. Suddenly a streak of lightning flashed in the sky, followed by a clap of thunder. It struck an enormous pine tree. Snap! Crash! The tree fell on a power line, causing it to break and sparks to fly. A branch scraped their window. They scrambled to the floor as fast as they could. The television and the computer turned off. The power went out.

That was just the beginning of a very interesting day.

"Jason, are you okay?" Elizabeth whispered. "That branch almost broke the window! This storm seems so strange to me!"

"Yes," said Jason. "I don't like this storm. Let's hope it goes away soon!"

It was a strange storm indeed. The wind sent leaves soaring into the air and twirling to the ground. The sky was a dark pink color and the raindrops sparkled with each flash of lightning. Thunder roared a bit more than storms they experienced in the past. Something seemed different about it. Even worse, they had no power.

Jason pouted. "What are we going to do now? No television, no computer. What else is there?"

Mom was in the kitchen, making lunch. She heard them and replied. "It's okay kids, the weather forecast says the storm will be over soon. I called the electric company to let them know about the broken line. Hey! This is a great opportunity for you to find something to do without electricity. Unplug and use your imagination. Won't that be fun?"

Jason began to think. Fun? Use my imagination? What does mom mean by that? "Mom, just what do you mean? What is imagination?" He asked.

His mom replied. "Imagination is something you create in your mind. It's not a real thing. It is make believe, so you can make anything up. That would be my explanation. Why don't you give it a try?"

Fortunately they still had daylight so they could see without lights.

So, they went from room to room searching for their imagination. They looked in the bedroom, the living room, and the kitchen, but they couldn't find anything that would spark their imagination.

As they approached the laundry room, lightning flashed so bright it made them stop in the doorway. They peered into the room and there it was. On a shelf, just above the washing machine, sat a purplish, greenish, glittering box.

Elizabeth gasped, "Jason, what's that?"

Elizabeth stayed behind Jason as they slowly entered the room. The purplish, greenish box glistened and wiggled as it sprayed a little bit of glitter on the floor. The closer they got to it, the more it wiggled. It wiggled so much it fell off the shelf and landed right in front of them. When it hit the floor, its top sprang open like a jack in the box. They both jumped back and ran out the door. They peered back into the room through the doorway.

"What's in it?" Elizabeth asked. "Let's go look. You go first."

Jason planted his feet on the floor and stretched his neck as far as he could. He peered into the box and sighed, "it's empty."

What do you think they expected to see in the box?

The wind howled and lightning flashed through the room. Thunder rumbled and shook the house. The box quivered then, bounced up and down. It opened and closed a few times then molded into a long gray tube. Wings with flaps pushed out of both sides. Inside the tube, a steering wheel popped out of a dashboard that was lit up with gauges. Rubbery, green seats with handles rose up from the bottom. Then a door appeared on the side and swung open as if it were inviting them in. In bright green letters the words TIME FOR A RIDE appeared on the dashboard.

"It's a rocket!" Jason screamed with excitement. "Let's get in!"

Elizabeth and Jason jumped into the seats of the transformed box. Seatbelts rolled out from behind and safely strapped them in. The walls of the laundry room turned into blue sky and puffs of cottony clouds appeared. The plane's engines roared and up they went, straight up then straight down at a very fast speed. They held onto the handles as the rocket circled and spun around the room. Faster and faster they soared and then the dashboard lit up with the words PREPARE FOR LANDING in bright green letters. As they approached the floor, the rocket slowed. The engines hummed and the words NOW LANDING lit up the dash in bright yellow letters. The rocket turned itself upright and landed safely. The engines mumbled and the rocket positioned itself on its side so the kids could get out. The seatbelts popped off and the seats filled up like balloons and bounced them out. The clouds and sky disappeared and the rocket turned back into the box.

"Wow!" Jason yelled with excitement. "That was so much fun!"

Elizabeth was a bit overwhelmed. "I would rather be in the snow with a beautiful pony pulling a cozy sleigh," she said.

The wind raged and lightning flashed once again. Thunder roared. The box shook and sprayed more glitter on the floor. The sides flattened out and the front curled up to form a sleigh. Jingling brass bells attached themselves to the sides. Cushiony red velvet seats puffed up from the floor. Two shiny metal runners pushed the sleigh up from underneath. Long wooden shafts appeared in the front. Snow began to fall and the room opened up to an outside winter wonderland. A majestic white pony in a silver harness trotted up from a snow covered forest. Elizabeth reached out and hugged the pony while Jason patted her soft white fur. The pony swished her tail, winked at them, then backed between the shafts.

Elizabeth gazed at the pony. "She is beautiful," she said.

The sleigh began to complete its form. Foot pedals popped out of each side. Elizabeth and Jason put their feet on the pedals and climbed into the red velvet seats. Long golden ropes fell into their hands and a warm blanket covered their legs. Swoosh! Off they went through the snow covered trees, over a sparkling brook, then up a high mountain. Their cheeks turned bright pink from the icy air. The sleigh followed a long, winding path through snow covered trees spinning in circles at every turn. It whirled around so fast Elizabeth lost her balance and flew into the air. The long ropes flew into the air and gently wrapped around her, and pulled her safely back into the sleigh. "Awesome!" she screamed. When they got to the top of a hill the sleigh stopped. The sky was dark and full of shooting stars. Some streaked straight down followed by tails of fire, and some sailed through the sky sideways.

"Let's wish on a shooting star," Elizabeth whispered.

"Okay," Jason said. "But we can't tell anyone what our wish is, or it won't come true."

Elizabeth closed her eyes and made a wish. The sleigh began to move. "Hang on!" she shouted, as they slowly slid down the mountain. Before they knew it, they were back home. The stars, the pony and the sleigh disappeared and Jason and Elizabeth climbed out of the box.

What do you think they wished for?

"Where should we go next?" Jason asked Elizabeth.

"How about a sailing ship?" she said.

Once again, lightning flashed as the storm began to move away. The thunder quietly grumbled in the distance. Then, the box turned itself upside down and dumped glitter all over the floor. Its cardboard sides split open and formed into an enormous sailing ship. Salt air and fog filled the room. They could hear ocean water slapping against the ship. They heard the sound of boards creaking and the clanging of rope and metal fasteners hitting the masts. As the fog faded, a door appeared on the side of the ship. A long plank rolled out of the door and went over the water and onto the ground. Ancient barnacles covered the sides of the plank and bottom of the ship.

Jason turned to Elizabeth. "Should we go in?"

"Im not sure," she replied. "It looks kind of creepy."

Slowly, the door opened and a little girl walked onto the plank. She wore a long dress made of old cotton with lace and a frilly bonnet. She turned to them and said, "Hello, my name is Titania, what's yours?"

"Hi, my name is Jason, and this is my sister Elizabeth," Jason answered.

"I have a favor to ask you," Titania said quietly as if she didn't want anyone to hear. "There is a treasure chest in here," as she pointed to the ship. "But, it's locked and I can't find the key so I can't open it. Would you like to help me?"

"Wow!" Jason said. "A treasure chest? We'd love to help you find the key!"

He grabbed Elizabeth's hand as they ran up the plank. They approached the door and Titania brought them into the ship. The walls were made of old wood. Glass lanterns hung from the ceiling and cast off a dull light. The smell of seaweed and wet, old wood filled the air. Barrels full of apples and cider lined the back wall and sacks of flour and grains were piled up next to them. Shelves with blocks of cheese hung right above the treasure chest.

They got busy right away searching for the key. They looked in every crack in the floor, in the bunks and on the round rims of the porthole windows. They searched under sacks, barrels and shelves. As they were just about ready to give up, Jason spotted something shiny underneath the edge of the chest.

With excitement, Jason yelled. "Help me lift the treasure chest! I think I found the key!"

Elizabeth and Titania ran over and helped him lift the heavy chest.

"We found the key!" they chimed.

What do you think is in that treasure chest?

Suddenly, crashing waves started to hit the ship. It started to rock. They were tossed against the walls. Water started coming in. Elizabeth screamed, "It's time to leave!"

Jason turned to Titania and threw the key to her. "Come with us Titania," he yelled. "We have to go!"

"I'm sorry, I can't go with you. I'm your imaginary friend," she yelled back. "Don't worry, I will go back to your imagination, so I will always be with you!"

Elizabeth called to her. "Fairwell Titania! We hope to see you again someday!"

"I hope so!" Titania answered one last time. "Goodbye! Thank you for your help!"

Do you think Elizabeth and Jason will ever see Titania again?

The room returned to normal and the box was back on the shelf. Elizabeth and Jason watched it, waiting for it to move, but the box remained motionless. The storm passed and the thunder and lightning vanished. The power came back on and the sun was shining.

Their mom walked into the doorway of the laundry room. "Hi kids," she said. "It's time for lunch. Do you want to go to the park after we eat?" Then, something caught her eye. It was the box. "Where do you think that old box came from? Silly me, I thought I saw it sparkle," she said. "Maybe we should check it out."

Jason jumped up and hollered, "no, no, no! Please leave it right where it is!"

She looked at him curiously. Then, her eyes focused on the box. "Okay," she said. "Is there a secret in there? Do you want to let me in on it?"

Elizabeth and Jason just looked at each other and giggled.

They couldn't wait for another stormy day.

Printed in the United States
by Baker & Taylor Publisher Services